Chasing the Moon

Copyright©2014 Tyler James Massey
All rights reserved.

Written by Tyler James Massey
Illustrated by Somnath Chatterjee
Edited by Bill Scollon

Printed in the United States of America

ISBN-13: 978-1505904512
ISBN-10: 150590451X

The evening fast approaches,
The day is nearly done.
The busy people down below
Bid farewell to the sun.

No more work for the parents.
No more play for the kids.
For the night is soon coming,
With it sleep gently bids.

Lights go out in the houses,
    All slip into soft beds.
Be they man, fish, or mammal
    Time to rest weary heads.

Songbirds sing the final notes
Of their sweet joyous tune.
While in the East horizon,
Rises the lonely Moon.

Keeping watch over the world,
Which passes slowly by.
The silver Moon glows softly,
Across the cold night sky.

City streets are all empty,
Green forest and meadow still.
Boats knotted to their moorings,
The Moon finds nothing 'til...

He looks to the vast ocean.
With his luminous gaze.
And there he finds peering back,
His own sad glowing face.

He wants to be as the Sun,
  So warm, so free, so bright.
As dawn arrives the Moon decides
  It's time to leave the night.

Long night after each long night,
    Through all of his phases,
The Moon flies closer to the dawn
    As the Sun he chases.

Trading darkness for daylight,
  As fast as he dare fly.
Until one morning dawn breaks
  And both orbs share the sky.

With a wide smile he savors
The warmth, the light, the fun.
The Moon learns how great it feels
To be the lucky Sun.

Birds fly in the bright blue sky.
In parks the children play.
A perfect new home he's found.
The Moon decides to stay.

The Sun greets him with a smile,
As the Moon travels near.
"Hello, my nocturnal friend.
I'm glad to see you here."

"It is truly my honor,"
   The Moon replies in kind.
"Your light brings joy to the world,
   Your rays heal heart and mind."

"The whole world is a-bustle,
    When from above you shine.
I've admired you always,
    And wished your gifts were mine."

"The night is cold and lonely;
No more where I shall roam.
That's why I've come to join you
Day shall be my new home."

Between the Sun and the Earth,
   The Moon begins to pass.
He blocks out all the Sun's light
   As his shadow is cast.

All the people down below
  Marvel at this great sight.
The night has joined with the day
  And day becomes as night.

The Moon and Sun seem as one,
  So magical and rare.
During the solar eclipse,
  The sky is theirs to share.

As the Moon passes the Sun,
Sunlight returns to day.
The Sun's truly impressed by
The Moon's wondrous display.

"You have a most precious role,"
The Sun begins to speak.
"You bring my light to darkness;
Give all comfort and peace."

"Poets write of your beauty.
   You inspire romance.
I shine so bright those below
   Can only give a glance."

"The night is lost without you,
Darkness is all there'd be.
Think of all that would be lost,
If you stay here with me."

"Night's a very special time,
With your soft light so blue.
To say thank you, this whole time,
I've long been chasing you."

As they bid their farewells,
Toward dusk the Moon returns.
With a newfound excitement,
For his old home he yearns.

The stars sparkle more brightly,
Welcoming their old friend.
Young happy couples hold hands
As they smile up at him.

He sees all the life below,
   Not everyone's asleep.
So magical and peaceful,
   Night's a great place to be.

He looks to the vast ocean
With his luminous gaze.
And there he finds peering back,
His bright and smiling face.

For my family Thank you for always teaching me to chase my dreams. And never stop chasing yours.

Love always,

Ty

Made in the USA
Coppell, TX
10 March 2021